This Stargirl book belongs to:

_____

_____

_____

For Kalera,
with love and thanks xxx

First published 2013 by Walker Books Ltd
87 Vauxhall Walk, London SE11 5HJ

2 4 6 8 10 9 7 5 3 1

Text © 2013 Vivian French
Illustrations © 2013 Jo Anne Davies

The right of Vivian French and Jo Anne Davies to be identified
as author and illustrator respectively of this work
has been asserted by them in accordance with the
Copyright, Designs and Patents Act 1988

This book has been typeset in StempelSchneidler

Printed and bound in Great Britain
by Clays Ltd, St Ives plc

British Library Cataloguing in Publication Data:
a catalogue record for this book is available from
the British Library

ISBN 978-1-4063-3339-8

www.walker.co.uk

Stargirl Academy

Lily's
Shimmering Spell

VIVIAN FRENCH

WALKER
BOOKS

Stargirl Academy

Where magic makes a difference!

HEAD TEACHER
Fairy Mary McBee

DEPUTY HEAD
Miss Scritch

TEACHER
Fairy Fifibelle Lee

TEAM STARLIGHT

Lily

Madison

Sophie

Ava

Emma

Olivia

TEAM TWINSTAR

Melody

Jackson

Dear Stargirl,

Welcome to *Stargirl Academy*!

My name is Fairy Mary McBee, and I'm delighted you're here. All my Stargirls are very special, and I can tell that you are wonderful too.

We'll be learning how to use magic safely and efficiently to help anyone who is in trouble, but before we go any further I have a request. The Academy MUST be kept secret. This is VERY important...

So may I ask you to join our other Stargirls in making The Promise? Read it – say it out loud if you wish – then sign your name on the bottom line.

Thank you so much ... and well done!

Fairy Mary

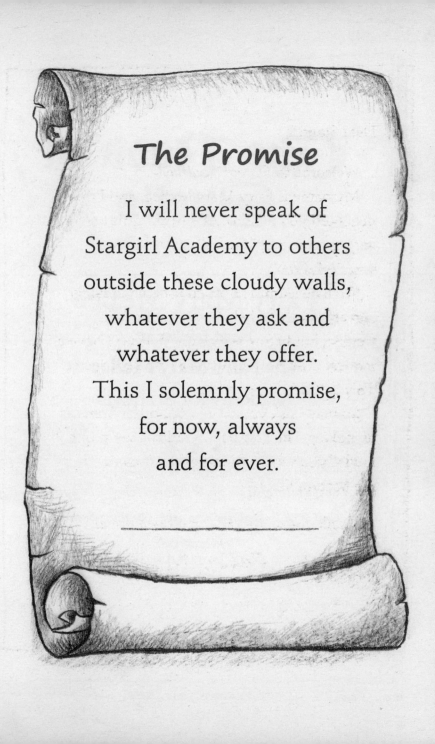

The Promise

I will never speak of
Stargirl Academy to others
outside these cloudy walls,
whatever they ask and
whatever they offer.
This I solemnly promise,
for now, always
and for ever.

The Book of Spells

by

Fairy Mary McBee

Head Teacher at

The Fairy Mary McBee
Academy for Stargirls

◆ ◆ ◆

A complete list of Spells can be obtained from the Academy.

Only the fully qualified need apply. Other applications

will be refused.

Shimmering Spells

Shimmering Spells are the simplest of all spells, and can be easily attempted by those with no experience in magic. The guidance of a professional Fairy Godmother is all that is required...

Shimmering Spells include such spells as:

- Floating objects in the air
- Curing bee stings
- Assisting cats from high branches

Hi! I'm Lily. Lily Henrietta Hawkins, and I'm ever so pleased to meet you. What do you look like? I have long, straight brown hair (boring) and not quite blue, not quite grey eyes. (Also boring.)

I don't know if any of you live with a great-aunt, but if you do, I feel really, REALLY sorry for you — at least, I do if she's like my great-aunt Acidity.

I was left on my great-aunt's doorstep when I was four. I don't remember who left me there; it wasn't my mum or my dad, because they'd vanished by then. They went to study a rare kind of butterfly somewhere in Africa, and they never came back. I suppose whoever was looking after me decided they didn't want to look after me for ever and ever, so they took me to Number 13A Dumbswell Street instead. I wish they'd asked me about it, though. Even when I was four, I knew about orphanages, and I'd have MUCH preferred to go to an orphanage. I'm sure they aren't nearly as bad as you read in those old books, and at least I'd have met other children.

But then again, if I'd gone to an orphanage, Fairy Mary McBee

might not have found me... and I
wouldn't have a story to tell you.

Love from

Lily Henrietta Hawkins

Chapter One

I sort of knew I'd put too much tea in the cup as soon as I'd poured it out, but it isn't very far from the kitchen to the living room and I told myself I could manage. I very nearly did. I got as far as my great-aunt's armchair – but then – OUCH! A tingle in my elbow. It was *really* sharp. And OOPS! – there was tea everywhere.

Great-aunt Acidity went green with fury. Her knitting needles flew in the air and Sweetypie yelped. It was awful. My stomach went cold and I felt sick. I was in SUCH trouble.

"Stupid child! Just look at the mess you've made!" Great-aunt Acidity grabbed

my wrist. Her skinny old fingers look dried-up and thin, but it really, really hurt. "That's your free time gone for weeks and weeks and weeks, and don't you—"

And then she stopped.

She was staring at something outside the window, so I looked to see what she was staring at ... and I couldn't help gasping. An enormous white cloud was floating by, just above the rooftops. It was definitely a cloud – but it looked exactly like a misty castle! A castle with hundreds of twisty turrets...

I rubbed my eyes. What made it even more odd was not the cloud being so low, but the fact that it was moving steadily along the high street, even though there wasn't any wind. Not even the tiniest of breezes.

My great-aunt let go of me and blinked. She pulled her glasses off her nose, polished them on the edge of my skirt, and we both looked again ... but the cloud was gone.

"Humph!" Great-aunt Acidity swung round. "What are you gawping at? Stupid girl! Can't even carry a cup of tea!"

"Stupid girl!" yelled Polly from her cage in the corner. "Stupid girl!"

 17

I stood on one foot and began to stammer. When I'm scared I can't talk properly. "I'm sorry, Great-aunt … I really am … I'm sorry … I really, really, REALLY didn't mean to—"

"Shut up!" Great-aunt Acidity banged her stick on the floor. "Fetch a mop right now this minute! And make more tea. With extra sugar. I've had a shock, and I'm a poor old lady who ought to be looked after. Not that YOU care. Little worm. Slug. Creepy crawly tiddly widdly Lily…"

I scuttled off to the kitchen. As I was filling the kettle, my elbow did that tingling thing again, and I stopped to rub it. It was like having a pin stuck into me, or maybe a tiny electric shock. I wondered what it could be. Did it mean something?

18

Chapter Two

I managed to get the second cup of tea to Great-aunt Acidity without dropping it. I didn't expect her to say thank you, and she didn't. Instead she sipped it as if it was poison.

"It's too hot."

I didn't say anything. If it hadn't been too hot, it would have been too cold. I never ever got it right.

"Go and get me a biscuit," my great-aunt ordered. "I want a chocolate one. And so does Sweetypie. And don't nibble the edges!"

I tried not to look guilty. I'd had a peek in the tin after breakfast because I was still

20

hungry (the bones left over from Great-aunt's kipper didn't fill me up one little bit). There'd been two biscuits left – and I'd eaten them both.

"I'm ever so sorry," I said as bravely as I could, "but there aren't any."

"You've eaten them all, you greedy little worm!" Great-aunt Acidity raised her stick. "Run to the shop! Get more biscuits! NOW!"

"But…" I jumped out of reach. "I haven't any money…"

"Stupid girl!" Polly danced up and down her perch. "Stupid girl!"

Great-aunt scowled, and fished in her old leather bag for some money. "Here! I want the BEST chocolate biscuits, mind. And you'd better be back before this tea gets cold, or there'll be trouble. Take Sweetypie with you. He'd like a walkies… Wouldn't

you, my precious ickle pickle fluffykins?"

"Trouble trouble trouble! Stupid girl, stupid girl!"

I made a face at Polly and went to fetch Sweetypie's lead. He growled, and snapped at my fingers as I clipped it onto his collar. He always does that, and I sighed.

"Sighing? What have YOU got to sigh about, Lily Hawkins?" Great-aunt snapped. "I took you in when nobody else would have you. I fed you, clothed and educated you! What more could you ask for?"

I didn't say anything. What was the point? All I wanted was for her to smile at me sometimes. Or give me a hug. Or even call me her ickle pickle fluffykins.

I hauled Sweetypie out through the battered old front door and across the road to Mrs Shah's shop. I bought the chocolate biscuits, and when Mrs Shah asked me how I was, I said, "Fine, thank you," the same as I always did.

"And how's Miss Acidity?" she said. "We never see her outside the house. She's lucky to have a pretty young girl like you to look after her."

"Erm …" I said. "She doesn't get out much. Not at all, really."

Mrs Shah gave me a lovely smile, and tucked a toffee into my pocket. "There. And give your auntie my best wishes."

She was so kind I got a lump in my throat, and only just managed to thank her. "Come on, Sweetypie," I said gruffly, and we went outside…

…and the road was filled with fog. Thick fog. Very thick fog.

I couldn't even see our house. I took a

deep breath and dived into the thick swirls of white. A moment later, I saw steps in front of me, and I stared at them.

What was happening? Where had they come from? I'd only just that minute stepped off the pavement...

"WOOF!" Sweetypie gave a sharp bark and dashed away as if he had seen his dinner. I was so surprised I let go of his lead, and he bounded up the steps and into

25

the nothingness of the mist.

"Sweetypie! NO!" I shouted, but he took no notice. I had to run after him. What else could I do? I jumped up the steps and there was a door and it was wide open – and I was just in time to see Sweetypie vanish inside.

"COME BACK!" I yelled, but of course he didn't. So I followed him.

Chapter Three

I froze in the doorway. In front of me was the strangest room I'd ever seen. It was full of shelves heaped with papers and odd-looking jars and bottles, and masses of spiky-leaved plants hung from the ceiling. Under the shelves were cupboards and the doors were literally bulging, the way your cheeks bulge when you're eating gobstoppers. There were labels on the doors saying things like *Wands for the inexperienced,* and *Sleeping Potions,* and *USEFUL DISGUISES.* Several battered old telescopes were hanging on the wall, and next to them was a huge golden clock – at least, I thought it must be a clock, even though it only had one hand and there were no hours marked on it.

I was so busy staring that I didn't see the two women in the room until one of them sniffed, and I jumped.

The sniffy woman was very tall and so thin she could have hidden behind a lamp post, but the other one was small and round and old and comfortable. She smiled at me, and I almost cried because she did it EXACTLY the way I always wanted Great-aunt Acidity to smile – as if she really, REALLY cared about me and thought I was one of the nicest people ever.

"Welcome to the Cloudy Towers Academy for Fairy Godmothers, Lily," she said. "I'm Fairy Mary McBee and this is Miss Scritch." There was a cough from the tall, thin woman – the sort of cough that means, "You've got something REALLY wrong."

Fairy Mary looked puzzled for a moment and then her face cleared. "Oh! Silly me! This USED to be the Cloudy Towers Academy for Fairy Godmothers. But we're coming up to date. It's now the Fairy Mary McBee Academy for... What did we decide on, Miss Scritch?"

"Stargirls," said Miss Scritch, with a distinct lack of enthusiasm.

Fairy Mary nodded. "Of course. Stargirls. How could I have forgotten? So, welcome to you, Lily! And I'm so sorry about your little dog, but he was being very naughty."

"What?" I said.

It sounded rude, but I didn't know what Fairy Mary was talking about until she pointed upwards – and there was Sweetypie, floating just below the ceiling and paddling his paws in a useless sort of way. He was looking very sorry for himself.

"JEEPERS CREEPERS!" I said, and that didn't sound very polite either, so I curtsied. Maybe it was a silly thing to do, but I'd never met anyone like Fairy Mary before. I didn't look at the other woman. She reminded me too much of my great-aunt. "Please…

Wands
for the
inexperienced
✗ ✦

Sleeping
Potion

USEFUL
DISGUISES

PLEASE can you tell me… What am I doing here?"

Fairy Mary laughed. "You don't need to curtsy to me or to Miss Scritch. You're here to learn how to be a Fairy Godmother—"

Miss Scritch coughed again.

"I mean, a Stargirl." Fairy Mary beamed at me. "That's why I sent you a Tingle!"

"OH!" I rubbed my elbow thoughtfully. I'd heard of Fairy Godmothers, of course, but what did Fairy Mary mean by a Stargirl? I wondered if I ought to be scared, but there was something about her that made me feel the opposite. I felt safer than I did at home. Even Miss Scritch wasn't exactly scary. More ... unbending. And just as I found the right word for her, she gave me a little nod as if she knew what I was thinking.

"Sensible child," she said. "You think we're mad. I'm not, but Fairy Mary is. She's decided Fairy Godmothers are out of date, so she's come up with the idea of training children to help people instead, and she's going to call them Stargirls." Miss Scritch looked sour. "If she can remember the name, that is." She peered at me. "Do you WANT to be a Stargirl?"

"Erm… " I didn't know what to say. "I don't know. What would I have to do?" I looked up at Sweetypie. "Would I learn how to do things like that? That would be AMAZING!"

"You'd learn how to sort things out for people. To make their lives better. Happier." Miss Scritch didn't sound as if she thought this was an especially good idea, but before I could ask anything else Fairy Mary interrupted.

"Lily will make a wonderful Stargirl," she said. "And as soon as Ava arrives, we'll take the two of them next door to meet the others – and then we'll be ready to begin!"

"Begin?" I felt a bit anxious. Fairy Mary

seemed like a lovely person, and I didn't want to upset her, but I absolutely couldn't stay. "I'm really sorry, but I've got to go. Great-aunt Acidity sent me out to buy chocolate biscuits and she'll be FURIOUS if I'm not back before her tea gets cold. And I need to take Sweetypie with me, or she'll explode. How do I get him down?"

Chapter Four

Fairy Mary gave me a reassuring smile. "You don't need to worry about time, dear. The moment you came through the door, time stopped. Well, it stopped outside Cloudy Towers. Oops! I mean, the Academy. You could stay here for a week and your great-aunt's tea would still be hot when you got back home. She'll never notice you've been away. Not for a second."

"Oh," I said doubtfully. It didn't sound very likely, but Fairy Mary didn't look like the kind of person to tell lies. "Is that... Is that magic, or something?"

"Of course." Fairy Mary patted my arm. "And if you don't mind, we'll leave your

 36

little dog where he is. He tried to bite Scrabster and I really can't bear to have the poor old thing upset. He's not been himself lately. We've been flying so low we've had a couple of bumps, and it does make him howl quite dreadfully."

I hadn't noticed the old dog lying under Fairy Mary's desk. When he heard his name he came out and licked my fingers. I scratched his head while I thought about what Fairy Mary had said.

"Flying?" I suddenly remembered the strange cloudy castle floating past the window, the one Great-aunt Acidity had stared at. "FLYING? Are you telling me we're in that cloud? The one with all the turrets?"

"Of course we are." It was Miss Scritch who answered. "That's why it used to be called Cloudy Towers Academy. Very convenient, in many ways. It means we can travel wherever we want to." She bent down to peer at me more closely, and the end of her long nose twitched. "Did you actually see the towers?"

"Yes," I said. "And my great-aunt did."

"Oh dear!" Miss Scritch looked at Fairy Mary. "That's NOT good. Not good at all. We must try to fly higher as soon as we can."

Fairy Mary nodded. "Perhaps I should send Ava another Tingle." She reached up and picked a leaf from one of the spiky-leaved plants. "This should do it—"

And at that exact moment, the door burst open with a crash. A pretty girl with straight dark hair came rushing in, tripped on the doormat and only saved herself from falling by clutching at my arm.

"Oops," she said. "Sorry! I'm always falling over things… WOW! Where on earth am I?" She stared round, saw Sweetypie floating in the air above her head, and began to laugh. "This is a dream, right? I'm dreaming!"

Fairy Mary stepped forward. "This isn't a dream, Ava, dear. And I'm very glad you're here. I am Fairy Mary McBee and this is my deputy head, Miss Scritch. We'd like to welcome you to the Fairy Mary McBee Academy for—" she paused for the merest fraction of a second— "Stargirls. Shall we go and find the others?"

Ava caught my eye as Fairy Mary led the way through a tall door behind her desk. "Do you believe any of this?" she whispered.

"No," I whispered back. "But I don't care. It feels like an adventure, and I've never had one before."

"Me neither," she said, and we followed Fairy Mary.

Chapter Five

The room we went into was really cosy. There was a roaring fire, several large sofas, lots of comfortable-looking armchairs, and the walls were covered with portraits of pink-cheeked old women. Three girls were sitting close together on the very edge of the sofa, and they looked... I couldn't think of the word at first, and then it came to me. Stunned. That was it. Ava and I probably looked exactly the same. Another girl was wandering round the room and she seemed quite at home. She was wearing lopsided pink spectacles, and I liked the way she grinned cheerfully at us as we came in. I wasn't quite so sure about the other two

girls. They looked cross, and were slumped
in armchairs with their feet on a low table.
Neither of them bothered to say hello.

"We thought you'd like to meet each
other before we begin lessons," Fairy Mary
said as Ava and I sat down, "and I thought
I'd tell you a little about the Academy." She
pointed up at the portraits, and several of
the old women in them winked at us, or
waved, or fluttered their wings. I hadn't
noticed the wings before. Nor the wands...

"Fairy Godmothers!" I thought. "They're REAL Fairy Godmothers!"

"They were all trained here in the Academy," Fairy Mary went on. "They learnt their magic and skills at Cloudy Towers, and have been travelling the world ever since, helping people whenever they can. But they're growing old and tired, and they could do with a rest."

There was much emphatic nodding from the portraits.

"So—" Fairy Mary looked round at us— "I decided it was time to find more Fairy Godmothers. We advertised for older women with an interest in magic and good deeds, but no one applied. It was very disappointing and we nearly closed the Academy down for good, but then I had an idea!"

Miss Scritch gave one of her loud disapproving sniffs.

Fairy Mary ignored her. "I decided it was time for a new approach. We're always telling each other that children are the future, so I thought, 'Why not teach children to help make that future just a little bit better? They think helping people is fun, and they're quick to learn – much, MUCH quicker than us old things.'"

Miss Scritch looked as if she'd eaten a lemon. One or two of the portraits frowned.

Fairy Mary didn't notice. "And then I thought, instead of Fairy Godmothers, why not girls? Stargirls! So you, my dears, are going to be our very first team. And there will be more of you, of course, once you're well settled." She held out her arms, as if she wanted to hug us all. "Isn't it a wonderful idea? And Miss Scritch and I have decided to call you Team Starlight."

There was a smattering of applause from the portraits, and Fairy Mary gave them a little bow. "Thank you," she said. "I hope you enjoy your rest." The old women nodded, then settled back into stillness.

"It's as if they'd never moved," Ava whispered in my ear.

Chapter Six

One of the cross-looking girls put up her hand. She was tall and thin, with very black hair, and she looked scary.

"Yes, Melody dear?"

Melody scowled. "I don't want to be in a team."

"Oh!" Fairy Mary McBee looked surprised. I saw her exchange a quick glance with Miss Scritch, but then she smiled again. "Well, if that's what you'd prefer, I'm sure it can be arranged."

"I don't want to be in a team either." It was the other cross girl. She gave us a despising sort of stare. "I don't mind being with Melody, but I don't want to be with the others."

"H'mm. I see." Fairy Mary sat back, and considered both girls for a moment. "How would you feel about that, Melody? If you and Jackson worked together?"

Melody shrugged. "Suits me. We'll be… What d'you think, Jackson? Twinstar?"

Jackson spread out her hands. "Whatever. Sounds OK."

"That's settled then. You two will be Twinstar, and Starlight will be a team of six – Ava, Sophie, Emma, Madison, Olivia and Lily. Now, Miss Scritch and I will leave you here for a few minutes to get to know each other, and then we'll call you back to the workroom."

I was pleased I was going to be in the same team as Ava, and I could tell she felt the same. The cheerful-looking girl with spectacles came to join us. "I'm Madison," she said. "Isn't this all utterly bonkers? But I'm liking it, all the same!"

"I'm Sophie." It was one of the girls on the sofa. "And this is Olivia." She nudged the girl next to her. "She lives near me. She's ever so shy, but she's nice."

Olivia went pink, and gave us an embarrassed sort of nod.

Ava nodded. "Hi, Sophie! Hello, Olivia." She looked at the third girl. "You must be Emma."

"That's me!" Emma was small and dark, with huge brown eyes. "I'm ever so pleased to meet you! Did you get a tingle in your elbow? Wasn't it weird? I still can't believe I'm here, because one minute I was walking down the road and the next … FOG! There was fog everywhere!" She turned to Melody and Jackson. "Did you get tingles in your elbows too?"

Melody didn't answer. She raised her eyebrows at Jackson. "Do you think we should stay? These kids are incredibly boring."

Jackson stretched and stood up. She was really pretty, with long blonde hair and big blue eyes. "Might as well. I quite like the idea of learning a bit of magic." She wandered across the room and sat down on the arm of the sofa, next to Emma. "Yes. I did get a tingle in my elbow. And yes. I saw the fog. But remember this, kid – you, and all your little friends – Melody and I were here first. That gives us rights. OK?"

We didn't have time to answer. Miss Scritch put her head round the door, and called us back to the workroom.

Chapter Seven

As we walked back into the workroom, Sweetypie began to whine. I looked up and saw he was sitting on one of the top shelves behind me. He didn't look at all comfortable, and I almost felt sorry for him.

"If you promise to be good, I'll ask Fairy Mary to get you down," I said.

He growled, and I decided not to offer to help him again. It served him right.

"Is he your dog?" Ava asked.

"He belongs to my great-aunt," I said. "She loves him to bits. She calls him her ickle pickle fluffykins."

Ava smiled. "And what does she call you?"

"Stupid girl, mostly," I said. "And so does

the parrot." I saw Ava had stopped smiling, and I didn't want her to feel sorry for me, so I pointed up at Sweetypie. "He's such a grumpy dog. It would be BRILLIANT if I could make him float in the air like that sometimes!"

Fairy Mary McBee heard me. "That was the Floating Spell," she said. "All quite simple, really."

Ava's eyes began to shine. "Will we be learning spells?"

Fairy Mary nodded. "Of course. You'll be learning a spell every lesson. There are six different kinds – Shimmering, Starry, Shining, Sparkling, Glittering and Twinkling. Shimmering spells are the easiest, and Twinkling the hardest."

"Please," I asked, "will we learn the Floating Spell?"

"That's one of the Shimmering Spells," Fairy Mary said. "The easiest level. You'll be learning that today."

I nearly fell over in excitement. Emma and Madison clapped their hands, and Sophie and Olivia nodded enthusiastically. Even Jackson and Melody looked hopeful.

"We'll say more about our programme as soon as Fairy Fifibelle Lee arrives," Fairy Mary went on. She glanced at Miss Scritch. "Shouldn't she be here by now?"

Miss Scritch sniffed. "Timekeeping is not one of her talents, Fairy Mary."

"You're quite right." Fairy Mary gave a little sigh. "I'll run up to the top turret and see if I can see her coming. Perhaps the girls would like to ask you some questions while we're waiting?" And she hurried out of the room.

Miss Scritch didn't look very thrilled, but she sat down on the edge of the table. "Very well. Is there anything you want to know?"

Madison put up her hand. "Please, will we learn to do lots of magic?"

"It depends what you mean by magic."

Miss Scritch looked down her nose as if she disapproved of magic of any kind.

"Abracadabra!" Madison waved her arms

in the air. "Pumpkins into coaches! Mice into horses! That kind of thing."

"These days," Miss Scritch said coldly, "magic is more a matter of adjustment. A little change here and a little tweak there ... you'd be surprised what a difference it can make."

Madison looked disappointed. "Oh," she said. "I was hoping I could change my big sister into a toad."

We all laughed, except for Jackson and Melody. They were sitting at the end of the table looking superior.

"Toads!" Melody said in an undertone. "How babyish."

"Who will we be helping?" Emma wanted to know. "Will we be going out all on our own to look for people who need our help or will Fairy Mary tell us what to

do and where to go? And will the Academy
be flying all over the world or will it—"

Miss Scritch held up a warning finger.
"That's enough, Emma. You must learn to ask
one question at a time. I do know that Fairy
Mary is hoping you'll work in your teams."

"Starlight girls for ever!" Madison was

grinning at us, her spectacles even more crooked than before. "We're a team now."

"Yes!" Ava gave Madison a thumbs-up. "Team Starlight is the best!"

Ava's voice was loud, and I saw Jackson and Melody look up from the other end of the table and frown.

Chapter Eight

I didn't have time to think about Jackson and Melody. Fairy Mary McBee had bustled back and was already talking.

"Fairy Fifibelle Lee is almost here, so I shall begin. Are you all listening carefully?"

We nodded.

"Excellent!" Fairy Mary stood up very straight. "So here we are, on the very first day of the first term of The Fairy Mary McBee Academy for Stargirls! I'm absolutely delighted to welcome you here. Welcome to you all, my dears!" She paused and after a moment Miss Scritch began to clap. We joined in, and we were far more enthusiastic than Miss Scritch.

Fairy Mary looked pleased. "We'll begin with The Promise, and then I'll present you with your necklaces."

NECKLACES? What kind of necklaces? We looked at each other in surprise, and Melody and Jackson began whispering to each other. If Fairy Mary heard them, she took no notice. "Every time you come here," she went on, "you will learn at least one spell. Once you've learnt it to a satisfactory standard, you will be expected to use it to help someone in need or distress. If you succeed—" Fairy Mary McBee positively glowed—"you will win something very special!"

Melody and Jackson stopped whispering and stared.

"Special?" Melody asked loudly. "What sort of special?"

Miss Scritch stepped forward. "You'll find out all in good time. Kindly let Fairy Mary finish."

It was obvious that Melody wanted to ask more questions, but Jackson elbowed her sharply, and she was quiet.

Fairy Mary tapped on the table. "First things first! It's time for The Promise, Stargirls. We ask you to promise NEVER to talk about the Academy to anyone outside. Everyone, please raise your left hand and extend your fingers like a star."

We did as we were told.

Fairy Mary McBee nodded at us. "Now, repeat after me. *I will never speak of Stargirl Academy to others outside these cloudy walls, whatever they ask and whatever they offer. This I solemnly promise, for now, always and for ever.*"

A little shiver ran down my spine as I

listened. I reached out to Sophie and Ava, and all of us in Starlight shut our eyes and held hands as we made our promise.

"Well done!" said Fairy Mary and as we opened our eyes again, a cloud of shimmery stars drifted down from the ceiling. For a magic moment, they clung to our hair and our clothes and our faces, and then they melted away ... except for a tiny, TINY

star on the tip of the littlest finger of my left hand. I stared at it.

"Do we keep them, do you think?" I asked Ava. "Even when we go home?" I loved the idea of having a teeny star of my own.

Ava didn't answer. She was too busy admiring her own star.

"Dearest Lily! You will always have your star, but once you leave here, you won't

see it unless you need it," said a soft voice
beside me.

I knew at once this must be Fairy Fifibelle
Lee. Her snow-white hair was floating round
her face as if she was surrounded by her very

 64

own gentle breeze, and she seemed to be hovering over the carpet instead of standing on it. She was dressed in so many long wispy scarves that I couldn't see where her skirts ended, but I was sure her feet didn't touch the ground. She looked kind, and I smiled at her.

"The stars are beautiful," I said.

"Indeed they are," she said, and then she was gone – and I saw her standing next to Fairy Mary at the other end of the room.

"She looks like a REAL Fairy Godmother," Sophie whispered. "She's even got wings! Little shimmery wings!"

There was a loud sniff from Miss Scritch. "Quite unnecessary," she said. "Nobody wears wings these days. Fairy Fifibelle Lee can manage perfectly well without them."

"But the children love them," Fairy Fifibelle cooed. "Don't you, my darlings?" She turned to Fairy Mary. "And what are we going to begin with, dear Fairy Mary?" She clicked her fingers, and a glittery notebook spun out of nowhere and into her hand. "I do have a few suggestions. 'Tact and Discretion' – SO important for a modern Stargirl! And what about 'Removal and Reversal' for when things go a teensy little bit wrong?"

"H'mph!" Miss Scritch muttered behind me. "Fairy Fifibelle Lee should know ALL about that. She's had more spells go wrong than I've had hot dinners!"

"And of course the darling girls should know all about history," Fairy Fifibelle Lee went on, "especially the history of Fairy Godmothers. And disguises. Oh, how I LOVE disguises! And what about—"

Fairy Mary McBee held up her hand. "Thank you, dear," she said firmly. "Your

enthusiasm is delightful, but Miss Scritch
and I have already prepared a timetable for
the girls."

"Oh." Fairy Fifibelle drooped, and the
notebook vanished.

"But it would be splendid," Fairy Mary
said quickly, "if you could teach them a
Shimmering Spell. Something simple –
perhaps how to float
things."

Chapter Nine

At once, Fairy Fifibelle was sparkling again. "My darlings!" she cooed. "It's the easiest spell in the world!" She twirled round to Fairy Mary. "May I show them right now this minute? Oh, do say I may!"

Fairy Mary's eyes twinkled. "Of course, Fifibelle dearest. Off you go!"

Fairy Fifibelle was almost dancing as she opened a large bag and took out a vase of flowers. Putting the vase on the table, she looked round to make sure we were all watching. "Point with your little finger," she said. "The one with the star. And think, 'Up! Up! Up!' Concentrate, now!"

"Excuse me!" Jackson leant forward.

"Don't we get wands?"

Fairy Fifibelle shook her head. "Very few of us use wands these days, my precious."

"That's because she always loses hers." Miss Scritch was still muttering to herself. "Any sensible Fairy Godmother keeps the same wand for a lifetime."

I was longing to ask her if she had a wand, but I didn't quite dare. Madison did, though, and Miss Scritch smiled grimly. "That's my business, Madison, not yours. Concentrate on that vase!"

Madison winked at me, and turned her attention back to the vase of flowers. The vase stayed exactly where it was.

"Try harder, girls!" Fairy Fifibelle drifted round the table. "Shut your eyes, and think, think, THINK!"

We thought, and we thought, and you

could hear murmurs of "Up! Up! Up!" filling the room. I half-opened one eye, and saw the flowers beginning to tremble … but then they settled down again. I hastily shut my eye and went on thinking.

"WOOF!" Sweetypie's bark was loud and indignant.

I looked up and gasped. "JEEPERS! LOOK!" And I pointed up to the top shelf. Sweetypie had one flower tucked jauntily behind his ear. The rest were in the flower vase beside him.

"Dilly dilly daffodils!" Fairy Fifibelle was so delighted that I suspect she thought we'd fail completely. "My clever, clever darlings! Let's see if you can do it again. This time try working in pairs." She fished in her bag and put four apples on the table. "Try these."

The apples were much harder. Ava and I worked together, and it took us ages and ages to get our apple even to lurch from side to side. Sophie and Emma got theirs to wobble up a centimetre or two, but then it fell back and wouldn't move again. Madison and Olivia couldn't make theirs even wobble.

Jackson and Melody, however, floated their apple right up to the ceiling.

"Some people have a gift for magic," Jackson said smugly.

"That's right," Melody agreed. "I don't know why you bother with those other kids, Fairy Mary McBee. It's perfectly obvious that Jackson and I are the ones you should be training."

I thought Fairy Mary might be cross, but she wasn't. All she said was, "Different people have different skills, Melody."

"That's right, my little petals!" Fairy Fifibelle waved her hands, and three of the four apples floated back to drop neatly into her bag. Only our apple stayed where it was. I was still staring at it and willing it to float; Melody was beginning to annoy me, and I was determined to make the spell work. I

stared and stared, and Ava edged closer. "Up,"
we whispered, and the next minute the air
was full of shimmering stars.

"YES!" we shouted, and a moment later
the apple was whizzing round and round
the room and we were having to duck as it
flew perilously close to our heads.

"We did it!" I yelled, and the rest of
Starlight cheered. I didn't look at Melody
and Jackson.

Chapter Ten

"Well done, Stargirls, and thank you so much, Fairy Fifibelle." Fairy Mary McBee caught our apple without even looking at it. She put it down, closed her eyes, and murmured a few words that I couldn't hear. The next minute, there was a huge apple pie with a crisp golden crust right there on the table in front of us. "I think it's time we had a lunch break," she said calmly. "Miss Scritch, perhaps you could rustle up a few sandwiches?"

Miss Scritch slid a wand from her sleeve (Madison was watching her with interest) and waved it a couple of times. There was a sudden bright flash – so bright I had to shut

my eyes – and when I opened them again
the apple pie was surrounded by plates of
the most delicious-looking sandwiches you
could ever imagine.

"WOW! If that isn't magic," Madison said
admiringly, "I'd like to know what is!"

"Help yourselves, my dears," Fairy Mary
said. "And while you're eating, I'll sort out
your necklaces."

At once Jackson and Melody stood up.
"We've been talking about the necklaces,"
Melody said, "and we don't want any. We
want to wear our own jewellery. We don't
want to be stuck with the same as all the
other kids." She gave us a despising sort of
stare. "And that's that."

Fairy Mary smiled as if Melody had
said something pleasant instead of being
horribly rude. "Are you quite sure, dear?

These particular necklaces are just a little bit special. They can help you to fade away until you can hardly be seen ... I would almost go so far as to say that in certain circumstances you could be quite invisible."

There was a long silence. You could have heard a pin drop. And then Sophie said, "Please, Fairy Mary ... did you say ... *invisible?*"

"That's right, dear." Fairy Mary was bustling about opening cupboards and drawers. "As soon as you give the pendant a little tap, you'll be invisible. Eventually you'll learn to be invisible by magic, but that really is a VERY advanced level of ability. Miss Scritch, I don't suppose you remember where I put them?"

Miss Scritch marched over and opened a cupboard marked: COACH POLISH.

"Oh yes! Of course." Fairy Mary leant inside and pulled out a small glittering box. She opened it up, and handed each of us a small blue velvet bag.

"Here, my dears. Use them carefully and guard them well."

I'd never EVER been given any jewellery. I held my breath as I opened my velvet bag.

Inside was the prettiest silver chain, and hanging from it was a pendant made of midnight-blue enamel, with the school crest of two crossed wands and six stars.

"Oh!" I breathed. "It's LOVELY! Thank you so much!"

"Tch! So you DID decide on the crest!" Miss Scritch sounded disapproving, and Fairy Mary went pink.

"I know they were expensive, dear, but look! You see the stars? Every time they do a Good Deed, a star will light up! And when they have won six stars they will be qualified Stargirls."

Miss Scritch didn't say anything more, but she still looked cross.

Melody and Jackson didn't say anything either, but I noticed them putting on their necklaces without a fuss. Ava, Sophie, Emma and Olivia were delighted with theirs, and Madison positively glowed as I helped her do up her clasp.

"You all look simply splendid!" Fairy Mary McBee clapped her hands. "Now, let's have something to eat."

Chapter Eleven

We ate every single sandwich and every single crumb of the apple pie. Then, feeling almost uncomfortably full, we got up from the table.

It sounds silly, but I had to keep looking down at my beautiful necklace. I'd never had anything so pretty, but I did wonder if it made my top and my skirt look even shabbier than before. Great-aunt Acidity never buys me new clothes; she sends me to the charity shops instead.

I asked Ava what she thought, and she gave me an odd, sideways look. "You look fine," she told me. "Really. I promise."

"What a bunch of pretty petals!" Fairy

Fifibelle Lee said. "Let's see if we can make the magic work. Use your little finger – the one with the star on it – and tap your pendant."

80

We did as we were told, and it was SO amazing! The moment we tapped the pendants, we faded away into nothingness. For a while we played at wandering round trying to see each other; you could just about see if you screwed up your eyes, but it wasn't easy. Then Ava bumped into me and sent me crashing into Miss Scritch, and she was NOT amused.

"That's quite enough!" she said sharply. "Kindly tap your pendants three times."

It took a couple of attempts before we all reappeared; Madison tapped her pendant much too enthusiastically, and disappeared twice more before she was able to join the rest of us as we sat ourselves back down at the table.

"H'mm. A little more care next time, Madison, if you please," Miss Scritch told her. "Fairy Mary McBee, we should be getting on if we're to finish today."

Emma put up her hand. "Please, Miss Scritch and Fairy Mary and Fairy Fifibelle, how long do we get to stay here? I know you said we'll arrive back home at exactly the same time as we left, but will we be here for days and days and days of Academy time or what?"

"Each time you come, you'll be here for a whole day," Miss Scritch said firmly. "And you'll find yourselves here at least once a week. You'll be sent a Tingle each time the Academy is open."

"But what if we can't get outside?" It was Sophie, and she was looking worried. "I have to look after my little brother, and sometimes I have to be at home all day—"

"No need to worry about that." Miss

Scritch sounded kinder than usual. "Just pop into an empty room. We'll make sure you can find us."

"Oh." Sophie breathed a huge sigh of relief. "Thank you."

Madison was bubbling with excitement. "And nobody will ever know we've gone? Truly?"

"Nobody." Miss Scritch stood up at the top end of the table. "Fairy Mary? Are you ready?"

Chapter Twelve

Fairy Mary McBee walked over to the wall, unhooked the strange golden clock, and put it on the table. "When Miss Scritch and I were discussing the best way to teach you to be Stargirls, we decided—"

"YOU decided," Miss Scritch interrupted.

"WE decided it would be best to give you as much practical work as possible. The quickest way to learn is to try things out for yourself. And you mustn't worry; nobody ever learnt anything without making mistakes. Miss Scritch and Fairy Fifibelle and I are all here to help. So, enough of me talking, my dears. I'm going to show you the Spin."

"The Spin?" Fairy Fifibelle clasped her hands together. "Oh, Fairy Mary McBee ... do you think our little poppets are ready?"

Fairy Mary McBee didn't answer. Instead, she picked up what I'd thought was the hour hand from the clock, and held it high above her head – and I suddenly realized it was a wand. A gold wand! "Wow! Look at that!" Emma breathed.

Fairy Mary gave the wand a wave and a shake, and a few twinkly stars flew round the room. Then she laid it back on the clock.

"Spin, spin, spin," she murmured in a strange singsong voice. "Who will choose? Who will it be? Whose destiny will change today? Spin, wand, spin..." And she gave the wand a quick flick to start it spinning.

The room was filled with a gentle humming and the wand spun round and round, so fast that all we could see was a blur … and then it began to slow down. Slower and slower the wand turned, and then began to jerk and jump as if it was looking for something, or someone. Twice I thought it had stopped, but off it went again, until finally it was pointing straight at Ava. The hum faded away, and the wand was still.

"Excellent choice," Fairy Mary McBee said approvingly as she picked up the wand and the clock and put them back on the wall.

Ava gulped. "Please, Fairy Mary, why was it pointing at me?"

"It's time for Starlight and Twinstar to do their first Good Deed," Fairy Mary said. "And the wand has chosen you, Ava, to decide what it will be. It can be

something very small, remember." She looked pointedly at Sweetypie, who was snoring loudly up on his shelf. "Why not choose something close to home? After all, we don't expect you to save the world on your very first day!"

Jackson was frowning. "Does Ava have to choose for us too? That doesn't seem fair."

"The wand might choose you next time," Fairy Mary said. "Then YOU will choose for everybody."

"Oh." Jackson sucked the end of her pencil. "OK. So what are we going to do then, Ava?"

Ava looked wildly around. "I don't know," she said, but then she nodded. "Yes, I do."

"Shh!" Fairy Mary put her finger on her lips. "Don't tell me. Tell the others. Miss

Scritch and Fairy Fifibelle Lee and I are going
to sit down next door, and have a little rest
and a cup of tea. Come along, Scrabster.
Good luck, my dears! And don't forget to
use your Floating Spell!"

Fifibelle looked disappointed. "Couldn't
I stay with the sweet little things?" she
begged. "You know I won't interfere!"

Miss Scritch snorted. She absolutely did!
There's no other word for it. It was hard not
to giggle as Fairy Mary took a firm hold of
Fairy Fifibelle's arm. "Dear Fifibelle," she
said, "I know how much you know about
spells, and there's something I've been
meaning to ask you..."

We all watched as Fairy Mary bustled
Fairy Fifibelle Lee out of the workroom.
Miss Scritch, looking sour, followed them.

As soon as the door had closed Melody

gave Ava a cold stare. "So what's your Good Deed, Starlight girl?"

"Bet I know," Jackson drawled. "You're going to help that horrid yappy little dog, aren't you?"

Ava shook her head and leant forward. "It's something MUCH better," she said. "We're going to help someone who really, really needs help!"

We looked at her in surprise. What did she mean?

"We're going to help... Ta da!!! LILY!"

Chapter Thirteen

I went scarlet. Everyone was staring at me, and if I'd known how to do a vanishing spell, I'd have done it right then that minute.

"LILY? Why on earth should we help Lily?" Melody obviously thought Ava was totally mad.

Ava folded her arms. "Because she needs it. Her great-aunt likes her dog better than she likes Lily, and she calls Lily *stupid girl* all the time. And she doesn't have any nice clothes. So we're going to help her."

Everyone went on staring, and my face felt as if it was on fire. I wanted to hide under the table. "Um," I said. "It ... it's not that bad. Really it isn't."

"And how EXACTLY were you thinking of helping her?" Jackson asked. "Going to use the Floating Spell to make her wicked old auntie sail away down the street and never be seen again, are you?"

"Of course not. That's just silly." Ava turned to the rest of us. "We're going to go home with Lily. We can decide what to do when we get there. What do you think?"

I began to panic. "I'm not sure that's a very good idea—"

Ava put an arm round me. "It's OK. We'll be invisible. Your great-aunt won't be able to see us."

"I think it's stupid." Melody pushed her chair back. "You chose to help Lily, so I suppose we'll have to do something for her, but I think we should just get her dog down from its shelf." She raised an eyebrow in my direction. "That'd be helpful, wouldn't it?"

I nodded. I wasn't entirely sure I could say anything without my voice wobbling. I was feeling very strange.

"Sorted." Melody linked arms with Jackson. "That's what *we'll* do, then. You lot can do what you like. We'll get the dog down. Someone has to."

"I'd like to help, but only if it's OK with Lily," Olivia said quietly, and I was surprised. She hadn't said very much, and I wasn't sure what she was really like. "What do you say, Lily?"

"Erm … I don't know," I said, and I was right. My voice *did* wobble. A lot. "It's very lovely of you … but I don't see what you can do."

"Then why not let us come and try?" Madison polished her spectacles, and put them back on with a flourish. "Like Ava says, we'll be invisible."

"Well…" I hesitated. A little part of me was thinking, Why not? Just supposing there *was* something they could do … wouldn't that be so, SO wonderful? I almost couldn't bear to think about it.

"Go on, Lily," Sophie said encouragingly. "Say we can. After all, what harm can it do if she doesn't know we're there?"

"We'll be as quiet as mice and we'll check everything out, and when we think of something to do we'll tell you and see what you say," Emma promised.

I took a long, deep breath. "Well …
maybe." And then I suddenly thought of
something. "But will the Academy still be
in my street? Doesn't it move around?"

"We can soon find out," Madison said.
"Shall we go and see?"

"Erm…" I said. And then, "YES!"

Ava banged me on the back so hard I
almost fell over. "Hurrah! And you DID say
you wanted an adventure!"

"What about getting back again?" Olivia
asked. "Are you sure we can?"

Melody sighed loudly. "We'll tell Fairy
Mary where you are. You'll be FINE."

Chapter Fourteen

It was still misty outside as we made our way down the steps and into the road. Ava, Emma, Sophie, Madison and Olivia had tapped their pendants before they left the Academy, and I was the only one who could be seen. I was carrying Sweetypie.

When Jackson and Melody finally managed to float him down from his shelf he'd been oddly quiet and very sleepy, and I was hoping he wasn't ill, or anything like that. How could I explain he was suffering from the side effects of a spell? And I'd put my lovely necklace in my pocket. I couldn't risk my great-aunt seeing it; she'd have asked endless questions. She'd probably think I'd stolen it.

As I led the way across to Great-aunt Acidity's house, I felt more and more nervous, and the nearer I got the more it seemed like a BAD idea. When I reached my front door I stopped. I was about to say I was sorry but I just couldn't risk making things worse – but then I heard Madison whisper, "It's OK! We're here!"

It was weird. I knew the Starlight girls

 98

were there, but I could only see them if I screwed up my eyes and stared really, really hard... And then I stared again. Were there five shadowy figures? For a minute, I thought I could see two more, but then I rubbed my eyes... It must be a trick of the light, I decided.

"Thanks," I whispered back. "Here goes..."

I'd actually stepped into the dark and dusty hallway before I remembered. The chocolate biscuits! I didn't have the chocolate biscuits! I must have left them in the shop. I turned to rush and fetch them, but it was too late. Great-aunt Acidity had heard me, and she was already thumping her stick on the floor.

"Lily Hawkins? Is that you? Where are my biscuits? My tea's getting cold. Come here this minute!"

"Stupid girl!" Polly had heard me too.

Sweetypie woke up with a jump, leapt to the ground, and hurled himself into the sitting room. I followed, leaving the door wide open so the others could follow me.

"Sweetypie! Come to Momma and give me a great big kissie wissie!" I heard a horrified gasp as my great-aunt held out her arms to Sweetypie, ignoring me completely.

"Little precious," my great-aunt cooed. "Did you miss your poor old Momma then? Would you like a biccy-wiccy? Lily! Give me the biscuits!"

"Erm..." I began, and my voice was wobbling. Even though I could feel Ava's breath on the back of my neck, and I knew the others were right behind me, it didn't make any difference. "Erm... I'm so sorry. I haven't got the biscuits—"

"WHAT!" My Great-aunt's eyes flashed. "Stupid girl!" She waved her stick in the air. "Where's my money, then? Spent it on sweeties, have you? Forgot all about your poor old auntie and decided to treat yourself to licky sticky lollies and fizzy wizzy sherbets?"

"No!" I tried to stay calm. "I left them in the shop by mistake."

Great-aunt Acidity's eyes narrowed.

"Why? Were you talking to people? Telling nasty little lies? I know you, Lily Hawkins! Telling folk I'm a mean old woman who doesn't look after you! I've seen the way they look at me, and I know whose fault it is!"

"No," I said again. "I … I just forgot them. That's all. I'll go back and get them."

"You'll make me a fresh pot of tea first," said my great-aunt. "And some toast. And a couple of lightly boiled eggs. And don't you go thinking there'll be anything for you, because there won't!" She glared at me. "So what are you waiting for? Get moving!" She waved her stick … and the stick went up, up, up in the air … and flew into a corner.

Chapter Fifteen

My great-aunt blinked. "What's going on?"

Sweetypie jumped off her lap, and began to bark – but then he stopped, and rolled on his back, all four paws in the air.

"Lily! Is this some kind of ridiculous joke?" My great-aunt was angry – but something had happened. Her voice wasn't nearly as sharp as usual.

The stick came out of the corner, twirled itself round, then shook from side to side as if it was laughing.

"Oh … oh…" I'd never seen Great-aunt Acidity at a loss for words before. "Did you see that?" she asked. "Did you see what it did?"

I didn't know what to do. Part of me

wanted to laugh, but the other part was in a complete muddle.

"Yes," I said. "I saw it. Erm … I'll put the kettle on."

Great-aunt Acidity didn't answer. Her eyes were popping out of her head as she watched the teapot rise in the air and float across the room. There was a giggle that I recognized at once. Madison! And then the tea poured in a steady stream on to the floor, swirling round and round in a weird kind of pattern.

Only it wasn't a pattern. It was writing.

Madison wrote, *Be nice to Lily or…* And then the tea ran out. My great-aunt watched with a terrible fascination as the milk jug followed the teapot and finished the sentence. *Be nice to Lily or you'll be sorry.* A couple of sugar lumps added punctuation.

Great-aunt Acidity said nothing. Her face was the colour of an old lemon, and she was breathing heavily. The teapot and the milk jug settled down on the tea tray, and I moved it quickly to the sideboard. I wasn't

sure how much more my great-aunt could take. I was beginning to worry about her, she looked so strange.

"Are you all right?" I asked. "Shall I go and make more tea?"

"No." My great-aunt's voice was a croak. "Don't leave me, Lily! Don't leave me!"

"But what about your toast?" I asked. "And your boiled eggs?"

My great-aunt waved a limp hand. "I don't understand!" she said hoarsely. "Why is this happening?"

I could almost feel Madison looking round the room for something else to write a message with. "There won't be any more writing," I said firmly – and gasped. Someone had tweaked my hair!

"Tell her," a voice breathed in my ear. "Tell her she has to be nice to you! Stand up to her or she'll bully you for ever." And my hair was pulled again.

"Ouch!" I rubbed my head, not so much because it hurt, as in disbelief. I was almost – but not quite – certain that the voice had been Melody's.

Great-aunt Acidity was looking at me, her expression a mixture of fear and astonishment.

"Has something happened to you too?" she croaked. "But you're such a good girl—"

I nearly fell over in surprise. I'd never ever had that said to me before – not by my great-aunt, anyway.

"Stupid girl!" It was Polly. "Stupid girl stupid girl stu—" She stopped so suddenly that my aunt and I swung round to see what had happened. The cage had been covered by a rug.

Great-aunt Acidity moaned faintly, and
Sweetypie trotted over and licked her
hand. I thought she'd be pleased, but she
hardly noticed. "The writing! Lily! What
did it mean?"

I looked at my great-aunt, and I saw she was terrified. I'd never seen her anything other than cross, or angry, or absolutely furious before, and for the first time I realized that she wasn't a complete monster. She was just an old woman. And she looked … I don't know. Hollow. As if all that kept her going was being horrid, and now that had been knocked out of her, there was nothing left.

"I think—" I began, and my arm was pinched by invisible fingers. "That is … I know what it means. It's saying…" I hesitated.

"Go on," urged the voice, and I knew for sure it was Melody. "Go on. Before she stops being scared."

"It means what it says. That you should be nice to me." I spoke as loudly and clearly as I could. I went and fetched her stick from the corner, and tucked it beside her chair in its usual place. "You be nice to me, and then I'll be nice to you because I want to be, not because I have to be."

Great-aunt Acidity sank back in her chair, and I thought, "JEEPERS CREEPERS! I'm not scared of her any more." Her fingers were trembling as she peered up at me.

"I'll try. If I do, will the ghosts go away?"

I SO nearly said, "What ghosts?" But I didn't. Instead I said, "I'm sure they will." Then, before Melody could pinch me again, I added, "As long as we keep to our agreement, that is."

And then the doorbell rang.

Chapter Sixteen

I didn't know who to expect. I opened the door thinking there'd be nobody there, and it was just Team Starlight playing a trick. Instead I saw Mrs Shah beaming at me, a packet of chocolate biscuits in her hand.

"Lily, pet," she said, "you left these on the counter."

"Oh!" I said. "That's so nice of you!"

"Very nice." Great-aunt Acidity was right behind me, leaning heavily on her stick.

Mrs Shah handed me the biscuits and looked at my great-aunt. "So how are you, Miss Acidity? Your niece tells me you're not so well, these days."

"Not too good," Great-aunt Acidity said,

"Not too good. But Lily looks after me."

"Tea! Ask her to tea!"

Ava was hissing in my ear so loudly that my great-aunt heard. She nodded. "Quite right, Lily. A cup of tea, Mrs Shah?"

I could see Mrs Shah was astonished, but she was much too polite to say anything. She hurried through the door and into the sitting room before I had a chance to say I was sorry about the mess, but when I followed her the floor was clean. Polly had come out from under the rug, and she was looking ruffled.

"Stupid girl!" she squawked. "Stupid girl!"

Great-aunt Acidity made a tutting sound. "Excuse my parrot," she said. "She belonged to my brothers, and they taught her to say that." She cleared her throat. "I think they were meaning me."

113

I was so taken aback I didn't stop to think what I was saying. "But I thought Polly meant ME!"

"No, Lily." Great-aunt Acidity shook her head. "Me." She paused. "And perhaps they were right. Now, would you put the kettle on for us?" She paused again. "Please?"

As I skipped into the kitchen, I heard the front door open and shut, and wondered who it could be. I didn't have time to look, though, because the others were waiting for me. They must have tapped on their pendants because I could see them properly.

"Wasn't that just TOTALLY incredible?" Ava asked.

"What made you stand up for yourself like that?" Madison wanted to know.

"It was Melody," I said. "Is she here? I want to thank her."

Sophie and Emma looked at each other. "We *thought* someone else had come over the road with us," Sophie said.

"But we couldn't be sure," Emma went on. "It was ever so difficult to tell because we were invisible."

"Melody was standing beside me in your sitting room, Lily," Olivia said. "I could hear her muttering. She was very angry with your great-aunt."

"But that doesn't make sense!" Emma protested. "Melody's been picking on us and being nasty ever since she arrived, and I don't see why she'd want to help when she said she wasn't going to—"

"Maybe," said another, much older, voice, "it's because she's been nasty that she understands how bullies should be dealt with, Emma, my dear." And there was

Fairy Mary McBee, right in the middle of
my great-aunt's kitchen.

Chapter Seventeen

"Fairy Mary!" I said. And because I was too surprised to think of anything clever to say, I asked, "Would you like a cup of tea?"

Fairy Mary smiled at me. "No, thank you, Lily dear. But make your aunt's tea."

"We'll help," said Sophie, and Fairy Mary nodded.

"I thought you would. You've all been helping Lily, my dears. I'm proud of you. And I'm proud of *you*, Lily, for helping yourself." Fairy Mary's eyes twinkled as she turned to Madison. "Your Floating-Spell technique is much to be admired, Madison."

Madison blushed. "I was rather pleased with it," she admitted.

"I helped with the milk jug," Ava said.

"And Olivia and I made the stick dance," Emma put in.

"I had to keep tickling Sweetypie's tummy," Sophie said. "We were scared he'd bark at us."

"You all did very well," Fairy Mary told us. "Now, I think the kettle is boiling?"

Ava poured the boiling water into the teapot, and put it back on the teatray. Olivia arranged the chocolate biscuits on a plate, and I carefully carried the tray into the sitting room. As I came through the door, I remembered how the Tingle had caught me, and I hesitated. It seemed as if that had happened ages and AGES ago, but in real time it can't have been more than about half an hour...

"Careful, Lily dear!"

I nearly dropped the whole tray. Great-aunt Acidity had called me "dear"!

"Put it down near me, Lily. I'll pour out ... but you haven't brought a cup for yourself. Or a plate. Wouldn't you like a chocolate biscuit?"

I did my very best not to look like a startled fish. "Thank you," I said. "I'll—I'll go and get a cup." And I hurtled out to the kitchen.

Fairy Mary was sitting in Great-aunt Acidity's big kitchen armchair, and the rest of the team were balanced on the table and the draining board.

"That seems satisfactory," Fairy Mary said. "Very satisfactory, in fact. I'd say that you've done your Good Deed to a full-star level, my dear Starlight. Look at your necklaces!"

She clicked her fingers, and as Ava, Emma, Olivia, Madison and Sophie looked down at the crest on their pendants, one little star shone out brightly.

"Your first star will be shining too, dear," Fairy Mary told me. "And Melody and

Jackson will have theirs." She glanced out of the window. "OH! My goodness! The fog is beginning to clear! That means the Academy is on the move again. We must be quick!"

I suddenly felt anxious. "You're not going to go back without me?"

Fairy Mary gave me a big hug. "Everyone's going home now, Lily. But you'll be back with us in no time at all … just wait for the Tingle in your elbow."

Ava rushed at me. "DEAREST Lily! I can't wait to see you again!"

And then we were all hugging each other goodbye, and there was so much noise Fairy Mary McBee must have made some kind of spell — otherwise Mrs Shah would have been rushing in to see what sort of party was exploding in my kitchen.

Chapter Eighteen

As I watched the Academy fade away through the kitchen window, I did feel sad ... but not for long. I went back into the sitting room, and Great-aunt Acidity actually smiled at me. A proper smile! And I had tea and chocolate biscuits ... although she did say I could only have two. But it's early days yet.

And that night as I lay in bed, my necklace on the bedside table beside me, the star on the pendant twinkled steadily, like a promise ... and if I put my left hand into the darkness under the covers and peeped down, I could just make out a tiny glow on my littlest finger.

"I'm going to be a Stargirl," I thought sleepily, and then I began to wonder what I would do if the Golden Wand of the Spin ever pointed at me ... and I fell fast asleep.

Which Stargirl are you?

Are you confident...

Confident

Do you prefer cats or dogs?

Cats

Dogs

Are you very chatty?

Are you clumsy?

Yes

No

No

Yes

Emma

Madison

Ava

Lily Hawkins

Says:
"Jeepers
Creepers!"
(A lot!)

Starsign:
Pisces

**Favourite
colour:**
Pink

Dreams of:
Gorgeous
dresses

Loves:
Hot Chocolate
with loads of
marshmallows

Stargirl Academy

One Token

www.stargirlacademy.com

Stargirl Academy

One Token

www.stargirlacademy.com

Stargirl Academy

One Token

www.stargirlacademy.com

Collect your FREE Stargirl Academy gifts!

In each Stargirl Academy book you will find three special star tokens that you can exchange for free gifts. Send your tokens in to us today and get your first special gift, or read more Stargirl Academy books, collect more tokens and save up for something different!

3 Tokens Bookmark

7 Tokens Star rubber

15 Tokens Set of star transfers

5 Tokens Sparkly pencil

13 Tokens Door hanger

Send your star tokens along with your name and address and the signature of a parent or guardian to:
Stargirl Academy Free Gift, Marketing Department,
Walker Books, 87 Vauxhall Walk, London, SE11 5HJ
Closing date: 31 December 2013

Stargirl Academy

A message from Madison

Hi! Did you like what I did with the teapot? I was SO pleased with my idea! Now you've read Lily's story, I really REALLY hope you read mine. I don't have a horrible great-aunt, but I DO have a big sister... and I bet some of you know what that can be like. Tricky!

And we learnt a really weird spell. I didn't think I'd ever get it to work properly! If you want a secret peep at the first chapter, have a look at www.stargirlacademy.com

See you soon!

Love, Madison xxx